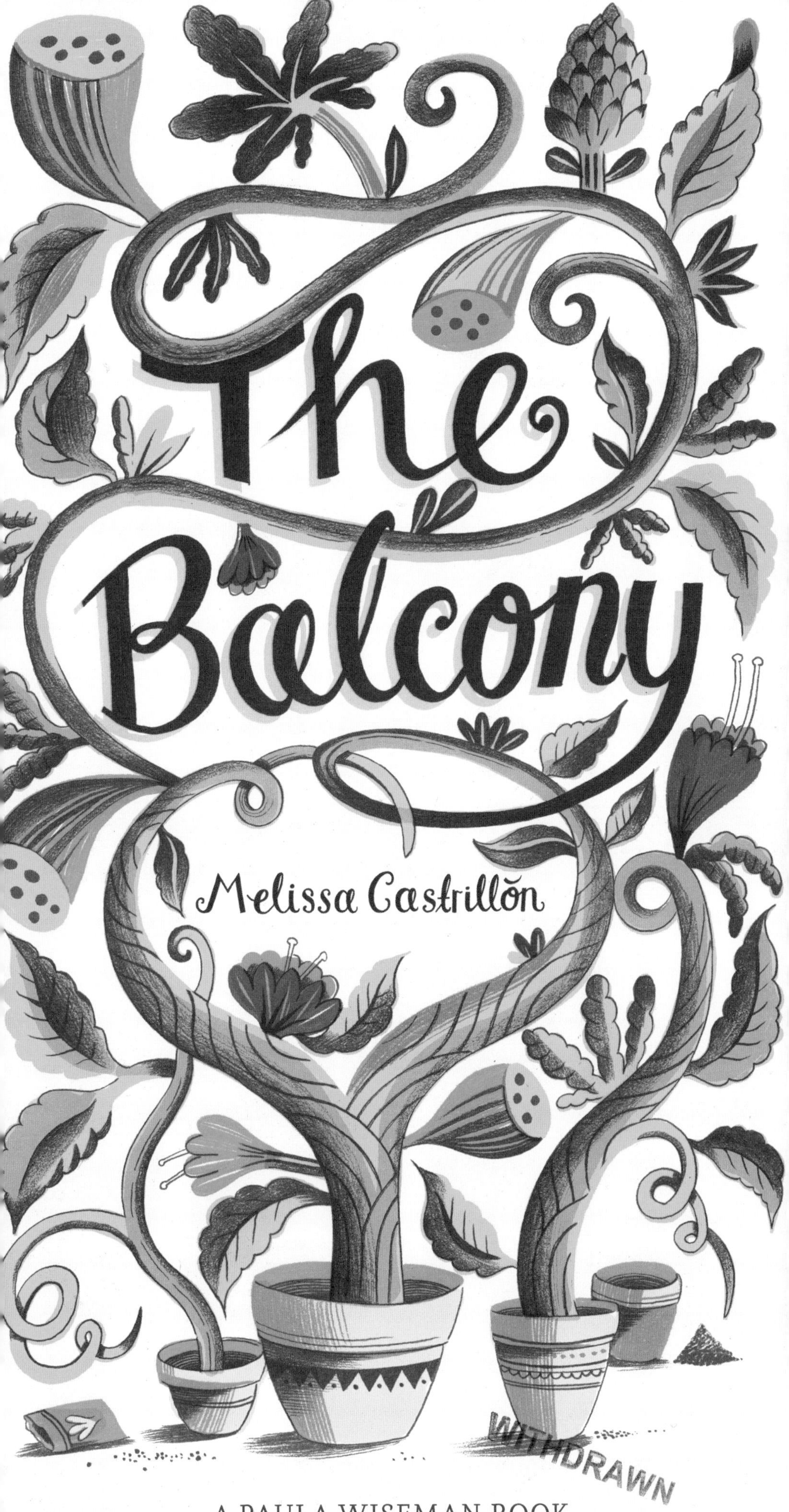

A PAULA WISEMAN BOOK
Simon & Schuster Books for Young Readers
New York London Toronto Sydney New Delhi

POST

Home
POST

Dear Mrs. Manrique,
Congratulations, we
Would love to offer you
the Job at our city office
and we look forward to
Seeing you very soon.
Best,

SOLD
Good-bye

SHOP FOR SALE

MY STUFF
MY STUFF

Hope

Bloom

FLOW
VACANT
OPENING SOON...

Hello

STREETFEST
ER SHOP
FRUIT & VE

Friends

Home

FLOWER SHOP

For Devorah,
my Berlin bestie, thank you
for all our amazing adventures
and for the one that inspired this story

SIMON & SCHUSTER BOOKS FOR YOUNG READERS
An imprint of Simon & Schuster Children's Publishing Division
1230 Avenue of the Americas, New York, New York 10020

For information about special discounts for bulk purchases,
please contact Simon & Schuster Special Sales at 1-866-506-1949
or business@simonandschuster.com.
The Simon & Schuster Speakers Bureau can bring authors
to your live event. For more information or to book an event, contact
the Simon & Schuster Speakers Bureau at 1-866-248-3049
or visit our website at www.simonspeakers.com.
Book design by Lizzy Bromley
The text for this book was hand lettered.
The illustrations for this book were rendered
in pencil and then colored digitally.
Manufactured in China • 0719 SCP • First Edition
2 4 6 8 10 9 7 5 3 1
CIP data for this book is
available from the Library of Congress.
ISBN 978-1-5344-0588-2
ISBN 978-1-5344-0589-9 (eBook)